Who's That Banging on the Ceiling?

Colin McNaughton

WALKER BOOKS
LONDON

First published 1992 by Walker Books Ltd
87 Vauxhall Walk, London SE11 5HJ

© 1992 Colin McNaughton

Printed and bound in Hong Kong by
South China Printing Co. (1988) Ltd

British Library Cataloguing in Publication Data
A catalogue record for this book is available
from the British Library.

ISBN 0-7445-2242-0

THIS WAY UP

For Françoise, Ben and Tim

Home Sweet Home!

"What's that clack, clack, clacking on the ceiling?" says Mrs Manky on the ground floor...

"It sounds like a dinosaur dancing the fandango!"

But that would be silly!
"What's that boing, boing, boinging?"
says Mrs Fettle on the first floor...

"It sounds like elephants on pogo sticks!"

But that would be silly!
"What's that spliish, splosh, splashing?"
says Mrs Dutz on the second floor . . .

"It sounds like a sea battle!"

But that would be silly!
"What's that grunt, snort, slobbering?"
says Mrs Gowk on the third floor...

"It sounds like a pigsty!"

"What's that squeak, squeak, squeaking?"
says Mr Clarts on the fourth floor...

But that would be silly!

"It sounds like giant mice!"

But that would be silly!
"What's that crash, boom, twanging?"
says Mrs Tarly-Toot on the fifth floor...

"It sounds like a rock and roll show!"

But that would be silly!

"What's that moo, cluck, quacking?"
says Mr Plodge on the sixth floor...

"It sounds like a farmyard!"

But that would be silly!
"What's that ow, ouch, yowing?"
says Mrs Haddaway on the seventh floor...

"It sounds like a fight!"

But that would be silly!
"What's that argh-ee-argh-ee-arghing?"
says Mr Chebble on the eighth floor...

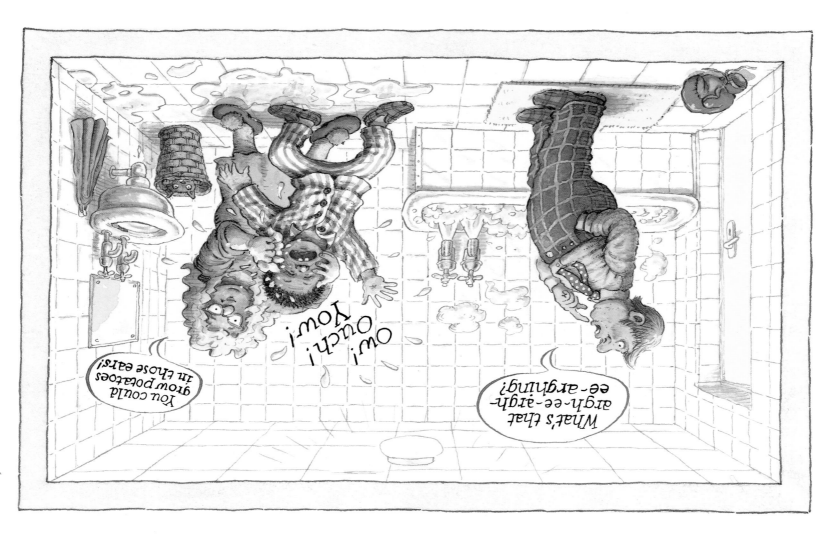

"It sounds like Tarzan of the Apes!"

But that would be silly!

"What's that huff, puff, puffing?"
says Mrs Gadget on the ninth floor...

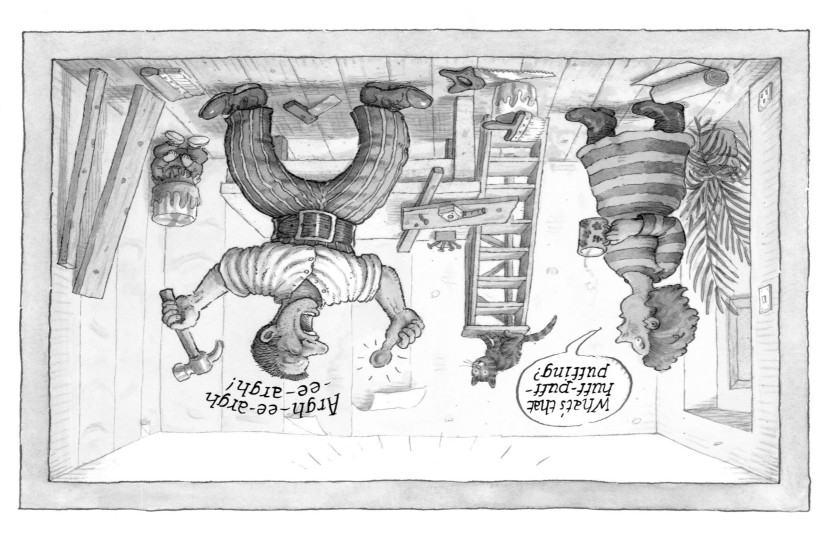

"It sounds like the big bad wolf!"

But that would be silly!
"What's that zap, bleep, blooping?"
says Mr Dunch on the tenth floor…

"It sounds like an alien invasion!"

But that would be silly!
"Who's that banging on the ceiling?"
says Mrs Hacky-Mucky on the top floor...

"It sounds like King Kong tap-dancing!"

The End!